A PEEK AT LOVE LETTERS

R.D. DAVIS

CONTENTS

FOREWORD

Secret notes passed to one another in class, longer notes exchanged during lunch and full blown "put it in the mailbox" letters were our pipeline to communicate. Mobile phones and texts were light years away from the late 1970's when we met. That's a great step back in sharing our thoughts with one another. No limits on word count, no hackers to break into our accounts and no prying parents to demand to see our phones. A pen and some paper and we were set.

We took time to process our thoughts just a while before responding to a question or situation that may have arisen. I found, over the years, that instant responses are usually written from raw emotion with no forethought of consequences and reactions. Not a good idea considering how easy it is to forward ecommunications to the world! A word of wisdom, no matter how you respond to troubling communications that you may receive… stop, take a deep breath and go get a snack. DO NOT RESPOND UNTIL YOU WALK AWAY FOR A FEW MOMENTS. THINK!

There is, however, a downside to putting thoughts and emotions onto paper. Some nosey persons could find them, read them and learn all about your relationships. That becomes particularly troublesome when a new boyfriend or girlfriend finds your stash of penciled love stories and doesn't tell you. I am certain that many heated discussions were kindled and set ablaze by the new found revelations.

The flames of love could either be ignited or extinguished by a love letter. Magical smiles could suddenly appear or streams of tears could begin their journey down a cheek. These letters could bring tears of sorrow or tears of joy. Smiles may be born out of a sense of relief as well. It's the same with tears, we cry because we are sad just as we shed tears when we are moved with joy. The written word is a powerful tool, particularly if someone takes the time and effort to join words and paper with their own hands.

This book is comprised of notes and letters sent between a real couple. Their names have been changed to protect their privacy. The timelines and incidents are real. Everything from their initial meeting in high school until just after they said, "I do," actually occurred. They are still married and even more in love. You may be asking "Does Alan realize what a jerk he was to Molly?"

I asked him and he does!

CHAPTER ONE

Molly,

I know that we shouldn't write notes to each other in class. You probably don't remember me but we were in class together during the first period. I wanted to see if you are OK after you fainted in class yesterday. It looked like you hit the floor pretty hard, I hope you didn't get hurt. Maybe we can walk to class together one day this week.

Alan

CHAPTER TWO

Alan,

I saw you looking my way that morning, so I know who you are. We had something happen in my family and I was up all night. My body felt like it just shutdown and next thing I knew the teacher was trying to wake me up. That was embarrassing. Someone said that I was high when I came to school and that was why I fell out. Maybe I'll go pop him on the head with my algebra book. I would like to walk to class with you tomorrow. Gotta go, teacher heading this way.

Molly

MOLLY,

I hope you didn't see my face turn red when Joanne introduced us today at lunch. Sometimes I'm shy but I'm glad that she did what she did. Being on the smoking patio with you was great. It was a great place to talk even though I don't think I said much, at least not what I wanted to say to you. By the way, I love your hair!

Alan

HEY ALAN,

Thanks for walking to gym class with me today. It was nice to have someone to talk with who is not so serious all the time! Are you always like that? Laughing with you was fun, I hope that we can do it again sometime. About hair, thank you for the compliment. You have great hair too, are you going to let it grow past your shoulders? One of my friends said that you look like an Indian and I agreed with her. I noticed that when we walked together that you walked behind me for a little while. I'm curious about why you did that. Not complaining but I would be saying something to you and you would just stop while I kept on walking!

Molly

CHAPTER THREE

Hey girl, how was your day? Other people told me that with my hair this long I look like an Indian. That's a great compliment, thank you. From now on when people ask about that I'm just going to say that I might be from the Cherokee Tribe. It won't be a lie if I use the word "might". If they ask about my ancestors I'm going to start telling them that I was raised by wolves and walk away. That will keep them guessing. Oh yeah, I would stop walking just because I was wondering about something and had to see for myself.

I HAVE to tell you that I really like you. You're funny, pretty and you laugh at my dumb jokes. Would it be okay to ask you to go out with me one day? If you have to ask your Mom and Dad, I get it. I hope that they say yes. Do you think that they will want to meet me first? If they do, I can always ride my bike to your house. I like you a lot. Hope your parents will let us go out,

Alan

CHAPTER FOUR

Hey Alan!

You like me. It felt strange to read those words. A good kind of strange. Why don't you just come to my house to see me? No, I did not ask Mom about us going out. Maybe I'm just a big chicken. There's plenty for us to do here even if we just go for a walk. Saturday or Sunday afternoon would be great.

Molly

DEAR ALAN,

I was glad that you were able to come to my house on Sunday. It was a good day but you left me confused and a little bit sad. I thought that it would be easier to explain with a letter. Perhaps we can talk about this later, but not right now.

We spent most of the day together, went in the field laid in the tall grass looking at the clouds and everything seemed to be going great. When you kissed me I was surprised and shocked, that kind of snuck up on me. It was great though, I'm glad that my parents couldn't see us.

Here's where you confused me. After the kiss you told me that, "You'll make a good wife for some man." What did you mean by that? That night I spent a long time trying to figure you out but I still don't understand. It didn't seem to bother you. Help me to figure that out. Please.

Molly

MOLLY,

Sitting to talk with you made me realize that I hurt you. I had no idea until then and after reading your letter. As I told you, there is no way that I can really explain why I said that. They were just words that passed my lips before I realized what I was saying. Maybe I'm just ignorant sometimes.

There is something different and unique about you, I just can't describe what that is. Hopefully I will be able to explain that to you someday soon, just know that it is a good feeling!

. . .

MAYBE WE CAN GO to a park or something this weekend. Being alone with you is like we're in our own world and nobody can bother us there. Did that sound dumb? Sorry if it did.

SEE YOU AT SCHOOL,

Alan

CHAPTER FIVE

Alan,

I thought about you today. Yevgeny Yevtushenko wrote a poem called "Colours" and it is in his book "Love Poems". Maybe we can read it together sometime and I can tell you why it brought you to mind. He's my favorite poet even though he's hard to understand sometimes. He is from Russia and maybe he just thinks differently than I do. I still like to read his works. Hey, I'm working on something for you, I should be finished in a few days.

SATURDAY WAS WONDERFUL! I'm glad that we went walking on the railroad tracks. It seemed like we were in an entirely different space while we walked and talked. I love being with someone who still knows how to have fun!

. . .

I SHOULD PROBABLY APOLOGIZE AGAIN for laughing when you fell down the hill. It was just so funny that one moment you were way up by the train tracks and the next you were on your way down. Your feet were up in the air and then your head and then your feet and then your head. An Olympic gymnast could not have pulled off that performance any better. I'll have to score you with all 10's in that event.

WHEN YOU STOPPED TUMBLING at the bottom of the hill I thought that you were hurt. You couldn't see me but I was laughing while I ran over to see if you were okay. Your whole body was still and I thought you were knocked out cold. To see that you were laughing so hard that you couldn't move made me laugh harder.

NO ONE, except family, has ever said,"I love you." to me. Just hearing you say those words was a moment that I will never forget. Telling you that I love you too was scary but the words flowed from my brain into your brain so easily.

I'll see you at school,

Molly

CHAPTER SIX

Hey Molly-O

The plaque that you made for me is incredible,I love it. This poet is new to me but I like his style. Don't know whether you planned it before we went to the park or after. When I told you that I loved you, had you already read this poem? Colours is beautiful!!! I hung it on the wall beside my bed so that it's the last thing that I see at night as I get ready for sleep.

Could you tell that I was nervous when I told you that I loved you? That was hard to tell you because I wasn't sure how you felt. Being rejected is something that I don't handle very well, if you had done that it would have been heartbreaking for me.

Do you believe in love at first sight? The first time that I saw you in class something happened inside of me and I got a funny feeling. Maybe that's what love feels like. It's just that I have never felt love before, not even at home and I have to try to figure out this feeling.

So, we've kissed and I told you that I love you but, I don't know where our relationship will go from here. This is hard to figure out. If we can see each other this weekend maybe we can figure this out.

One last thing. When I hugged you at the park your hair smelled like freshly baked cookies from your job at the bakery. I loved laying my head on your shoulder and just inhaling, I'll never forget that.

I love you,

Alan

YOU CONFUSE ME ALAN. Do you love me or do you not love me? You tell me that you do but then you don't act like it sometimes. One night I go to bed happy and another night I'm sad. It all depends on whether you love me that day or not! My Mom even notices the difference and wants to know why I'm upset. What should I say to her? Do I tell her that you just can't decide whether you like me or love me or whatever?

Molly

CHAPTER SEVEN

Molly

It's like I told you on the phone, I'm confused about relationships and life in general myself. Nothing makes much sense. My feelings for you are new to me, a whole new sensation. Maybe aliens took over my mind and I am under their control. Kidding! You won't understand this but part of me is just afraid to follow my feelings. Your parents are great, mine not so much. The house that you live in is big and it has lots of land with it. There are days when I wonder if we can even afford payments on our house. You drive your parents' new car and I drive clunkers. Your parents treat you differently than mine treat me. A big part of your life revolves around church while we never go to church. Youth groups would be a great place to hang out with friends if any of my friends went to church. Maybe I'm just intimidated by all that you have. There is no way I can measure up to that life. I think that you are way out of my league and you can do better than me.

Excuses are all that I have mentioned and I know that is not what you need from me. My brain just can't explain how I feel about you. My life has been drifting around from girlfriend to girlfriend. You are better than that and deserve much more.

I'm sorry, Alan

CHAPTER EIGHT

Dear drifter,

What? You don't make any sense with what you wrote. I thought that we could get together and talk through this but I never see you at school anymore. My Mom won't let me call boys so I just have to wait for you to call me. Your call never comes and I don't dare disobey Mom. When you get this letter at least write me back if you won't call me. Maybe you can find me at school and we can talk during lunch period or after school. I miss you.

Molly

CHAPTER NINE

Molly,

Today is a day that I will never forget and I hope that it stays in your heart as well. As we were walking down the greenway area a wave of emotion swept over me. Wish that I had a name for it, but it was a wonderful sensation.

That moment is when we stopped and just plopped ourselves down by the trail. Your eyes were an exact match of the blue sky. Those tall golden flowers just kept dancing around us in the breeze, almost as if they were inviting us to join in their dance. Your hands were soft and silky as they tightly held mine. That day could have been our last day on Earth and my life would have been complete.

Then we kissed. It was unlike any other kiss that I've known. The feeling is indescribable, I just don't have command of the words to fully explain what I felt. You rose ever so slightly to bring us closer together and then, it was over. My head and my heart were in a race to see which could beat the strongest. Then, as if the clouds moved away from the sky, you opened your eyes. We just sat there, almost hypnotized, and could do nothing but gaze upon one another. At that moment I had never seen anyone look as beautiful as you were. The whole world seemed to stop for us during the short time that we were there. We just sat and basked in the warmth of our love for one another.

Molly, I may be confused and my brain a bit scrambled, but those moments will be forever etched into my heart. I love you.

ALAN,

That day was unreal! It was perfect with just you and me with no one else around. When we sat down among the dancing flowers we couldn't see the rest of the world. It was as though there was no one within a hundred miles of us and that was a wonderful feeling. Please call me on Sunday when I get back from vacation.

Love, Molly

CHAPTER TEN

Alan,

It was great to see you and know that you were back in school. When you told me that you "just quit coming to school" I was shocked and sad. Who does that? You are smart, I have seen that first hand. Even talking to you I can tell that you have a high IQ just by the words that you use and the way you explain things to me. Please don't leave school like that again, please. The least that you can do is tell me so that we can work through your problems together.

When I told you about my marriage dream I wasn't sure how you would react. Like I said on the school lawn, my Great Grandmother told me that I would marry you someday. I believe her. I wish that I knew why she was able to tell me that, it was all so real. Your smile when I told you about the dream was priceless. I really believe that one day we will be married! You took me by surprise when you kissed me then. Just a sweet small kiss, but it felt wonderful. When you held my hand all the way to meet my Mom at her car and I felt wanted and special to you.

Alan I only know how to be honest with people and sometimes that hurts. You know my friend Rita. You have been in school with her since 1st Grade.

Hearing you say, "I love you Molly" is the sweetest thing that anyone can say to me. I know about that other girl that you have been dating, you slipped up in one of our conversations. Two and two added up pretty quickly after that. Anyway she and Rita are at the same school and your new friend talks when they are together. Alan, I've never been called such horrible names before...ever! A "slut" and a "whore", really? There were other choice words flung about but those two shocked me most.

That girl doesn't even know me, I've never met her. Perhaps I could say evil things about her but, I won't stoop that low. This probably takes you by surprise and hurts you and I'm sorry for that. You just need to know what is going on behind your back. I can give you Rita's phone number if you would like to speak to her.

Hopefully you can get schoolwork caught up in Summer School and come back to a regular school life in September. I'm here to help you if you need me. We can spend more time together this summer when my family gets back from vacation. We're due back on Saturday night, will you call me on Sunday afternoon?

You know I love you,

Molly

CHAPTER ELEVEN

Molly,

Hi! I need to apologize for just disappearing like I did. To just walk out of someone's life like I did is borderline meanness or at the very least just not polite. When you get back home, may I call you? My heart is sore from worry and guilt. Talking to you would be the greatest thing that could happen to me this summer.

My home life is just not a good place for education to be a priority. That takes a back seat to many problems that arise. I owe you an explanation for those statements, we need to sit face to face for that to take place. Missing you these past months occupied most of my quiet life. You are on my mind every day and it gets stronger when I try to sleep at night. There is just something about you and the way that I feel about you that I refuse to let go.

Explaining those feelings is difficult for me. I've never felt like this before and there is no one else that I can talk to about what I am experiencing . There is only you to talk to. I hope that you can forgive me for being an idiot and a jerk!

Alan

CHAPTER TWELVE

Alan,

I have been home from vacation for over a week now and you never called. When we got unpacked on Sunday I stayed inside waiting to hear from you, what happened? Surely you didn't just forget to call me or did you?

I was so excited that we could talk that my Mom noticed it. She and I sat down to talk about nothing but you! Now she knows how I feel about you, how we met, why I like being with you, and well, everything good about us.The question about why you did not call Sunday came up and I had no answer to give her. My bedtime came fairly early that night, I was sad and disappointed so I just wanted to be alone and quiet.

When you get this will you please call me just so I know that you are alright? I worry about you and miss you on top of that. There is a song that I heard last week that made me stop and think of us. It probably explains how I feel about you better than I can, I'm just not that creative with words. It speaks of saving time in a bottle and saving it for the one that you love.

By the way, I can't stop thinking about our day at the greenway park. Your letter went with me on vacation and I had to keep it hidden from my sister. She saw me read it and got curious. Alan, I have never been kissed like we kissed and it was incredible. Don't worry, I won't ever forget that day either, how could I forget it? It was one of the best days of my life. Just call me..please.

MOLLY,

Thanks for being understanding about my phone situation at home. When our phone gets shut off because the bill didn't get paid nobody gets called! You seemed surprised when I told you about the phone situation but I never heard any unkind words come from you. It was embarrassing to have to tell you.

Today when I just showed up at your house you had a great expression on ,your face. I decided to just hop on my 10 speed and go, even though it was a long ride. All that I wanted was to see you and no car was available at home to take me to you so, two wheeling seemed like the logical choice. I'm just thankful that you were at home and happy to see me.

You have become a great friend to me. Always listening, never judging, patient and understanding are only things that a close friend will do. Remember when I told you that I don't understand my feelings towards you and that what I feel is something that I have never felt before? While you were gone I thought about that a great deal and maybe realized what I'm feeling. There has never been a close friend in my life, in 17 years it has really just been me and no one else to share my thoughts with. Does that make any sense at all? It's the only thing that will explain the way I feel about you. I love you as my best friend and that is all new to me.

While I was biking back home the other day it all hit me. It was a whirlwind day and I think that I mentioned this emotional discovery to you. There was little time to explain it better, so I thought it was best to write to you before we see each other again.

DEAR FRIEND,

You make no sense at all and I just don't get it. When night time comes after we've been together for the day it's like we are more than friends. You have me totally confused. Loving me as a friend? What does that even mean? Do you kiss your friends or hold one another while lying on the grass at the park? I am emotionally strong, but you bring me to tears. The words that you speak to me and the words that you write to me just don't match. Why? That's all that I need to know is "Why?"

Your sisters must have told you that I have tried to call you. When they answered the phone they told me that they will let you know that I called. You even seem to avoid me at school. We never cross paths in the hallways even though we have classes close to each other. My friends see you and can't wait to let me know where you are. I won't chase you or track you down, that's just not my personality. Holly told me that I should just tell you, as she puts it, "Tell him to go to hell and leave you alone. I'll do it for you if you can't." Carol says that you're just mean to walk by the bakery while we're at work. I can see her face turn crimson red when you do that and you know how laid back she is. Then there is my Mom. A mother's natural instinct is to protect her children at all cost, nobody hurts Mom's babies! She has seen me moping around, red eyed and sad and I didn't have to tell her why.

I know that you are unsure about your feelings but I'm not. There is a question that I wanted to ask you when we were together last time but didn't think that it was my business. Your last letter made me realize that it is my business because I care for you so much. The big question is, have you ever felt loved by anyone? Parents, grandparents, girlfriends or really anybody? If not, maybe that is your problem with us. You just don't know what true love looks like and feels like and you don't understand how to give your love away. I may not know much, but I know what love feels like. Think about that friend!

We can sit and talk about it if you would like, but you'll have to call me and let me know.

Molly

CHAPTER THIRTEEN

Hey Molly,

I think that I picked a great place for us to sit and talk. It was good to be alone with no distractions. The fact that the lake was surrounded by summer sounds made it perfect. Hearing you,I began to understand what you were saying in your last letter. You are awfully patient to put up with me and the things that I say and do.

Discovering a great lack of love and affection in my life is astonishing, something that I had never considered until I read your last letter. You grew up surrounded by love, I think that I may be a bit jealous. What will my life be like in the future if I don't know how to love someone? That day is going to be a life changer for me and I must thank you.

We write so often that you'd think that we lived across the country from each other. I find great comfort in reading your words after having spent a day with you.

Telling you that I love you as a friend was pretty stupid of me and I wish that I could take those words back so that you would never remember them. One of these days I'll make that up to you.

Love you,

Alan

CHAPTER FOURTEEN

Alan,

As soon as I saw a pile of corn on our front porch I knew that you had to be involved somehow! You told me the other night that you and your friends go out in the country and "borrow produce" from farms. When you told me that part of me didn't believe you, but another part knew that it was something you would do. Oh, the corn tasted great! Mom wouldn't eat any ,though,since it was stolen. She asked me to thank you though. One of these evenings I would love to go with you and your friends on a veggie raid. Maybe we could just go alone and forget about corn!

I was with Holly last night and she told me about seeing you and Kate at the park. If you know Holly you must know that she was highly upset about that. She told me that, and these are her words, "I wanted to go over and slap the crap out of both of them.

What a jerk!" Everyone that we know realizes that you are dating her and spending time with her. Nothing against her but she just doesn't seem like your type. You're so mellow, laid back and nice. She seems to be the exact opposite of that. I know that she's not nice just because of the gossip that she spreads about me. It is a small world and I have a lot of friends that she talks with. It all gets back to me eventually. It's actually funny in a sad sort of way.

It hurts me that you see her, I wish that more of your time belonged to me. I've decided that I will date other guys instead of just staying at home all weekend. My heart is joined with yours, ever since that first day in 10th grade.

When our eyes met and we just gazed at one another, I knew. You know that as well as I do, you just need to face reality. Time has flown by since that day and my heart has never changed.

In one of your notes or letters, I don't remember which or when you mentioned love at first sight. Alan, I believe in love at first sight and that is what we experienced that day. Since that day I haven't loved anyone else the way that I love you. One day you will see what I am talking about for yourself. When you do I hope that you remember what I'm telling you in this letter.

Someone told me that you are missing a lot of days at school. I guess that's why we don't run into each other much. That makes me worry about you and wonder what you're doing all day. You know that I am always here for you if you just need someone to talk to. All you have to do is call me...and you know that. Please don't start wasting your life. You're smart and you have a great future ahead of you. You have told me about your family life, but you have to be the person to change things for yourself. Don't forget that.

Love,

Molly

CHAPTER FIFTEEN

Molly,

I still can't believe that you left the John Denver concert to just go ride around and talk with me. You made me happy, your friends were not so happy, but I was and you seemed to be. I'm sorry that I surprised you with my kiss when we got in my car. It had been too long since I had seen you and I missed you. My kiss was on your lips before I read what I was doing, it just seemed so natural and so right. The evening with you was nice, it was good to be close to you again.

I need to confess something to you and a letter is a good way to do that.Every day of my life, you are on my mind and in my heart. I wonder what you are doing or who you are with. I worry that you are with someone who is not treating you right. My imagination runs away and I ask myself what I would do if that happened. Being a gallant knight rushing in to defend your honor and protect you is a secret fantasy. When I lie down at night, you're on my mind. To be honest, sometimes at night I worry that I'll never see you again. I imagine that you've fallen in love (No one to blame but myself for that) and are going off to college with your new love.

My brain goes into high gear some nights and I even see you getting married to him. This sounds dumb, but I start to think of ways to stop the marriage. I've dreamed of just interrupting your ceremony or showing up at your house unannounced and pleading with you to not marry. My imagination never lets me win your hand and I just stand at the church watching you drive away into your new life. You can't imagine how sad I make myself on those nights. You deserve a much better man than I will ever be.

You know that I am still dating Kate but it's not the same as what we have and the feelings that I have for you. You were right in one of your letters when you told me that she and I are opposites. Our personalities, our wants and desires are just out of sync. I just can't see how this relationship will end, but it will someday soon.

I was listening to some music just before I started writing and a song came on that could have been written about me. It reminds me that I had a dream about us and you were lying by my side. All was right with the world during that dream. But, as with all dreams, I woke up and you were gone. Molly, you're my dream and one day I hope that we can wake up together. I don't know how or when, I just hope.

I love you,

Alan

CHAPTER SIXTEEN

Dear Alan,

Thank you for sharing your thoughts with me, they're special and straight from your heart. As for the concert, I would have gone anywhere with you that night. When I came down to the section where you were, your hug was so strong and warm that I didn't want you to let me go. I love just being with you.

A confession like you wrote is not a confession to me. After I read it I just had to sit and let your words sink into my soul. It's good to know that you feel the way that you do and imagine thoughts like those. To tell you the truth I can't imagine marrying anyone else but you. If I did and you came to sweep me off my feet I would probably go with you. The man I leave at the church won't be too happy and if Holly and Carol are there I can see them running after us to talk me into coming back.

As for your girlfriend, you are wise to know that it will end some-day. Oh, would you please ask her to stop harassing me? She calls all the time and then hangs up the phone when we answer. It has to be her, no one else would be calling my house like that. I think that I can put a stop to the calls, but I wanted to let you know first.

Molly

CHAPTER SEVENTEEN

Dear Miss Revenge,

I assume that by now you know that I was not angry when I called you Saturday night. The toilet paper hanging from the trees in Katie's yard was actually like a piece of art! That had to have been a good time, how many people helped you? Nice move!

Alan

CHAPTER EIGHTEEN

Molly,

I know that you haven't heard from me in a long time and I felt like I owe you an explanation. After almost 12 years of school, I called it quits. That's right you can call me a dropout. It's not as bad as it sounds though. I'd like for you to hear the truth from me instead of high school gossip.

Getting started with school this year was difficult. I was working nights and working too late at that. My brother and I had a job cleaning up a steak restaurant after it closed and the staff was gone. It was usually 10:00PM before we started and almost 12:30AM when we finished. I would get home, be in bed by 1:30AM. When the alarm went off in the mornings I started shutting it off hoping for a little more sleep. That was the beginning of the end sof high school.

Then in English Composition class everything just came undone. We were asked to write a paper about some song lyrics for homework. When I turned my paper in, the Queen, Mrs.G. brought mine to my desk. They had been quickly skimmed over and graded. Mrs.G. informed me that, "Alan, even you can do better than this." She had placed the work on my desk and then picked it back up. A trip straight to the trash can and my work was gone. That was embarrassing and bullying, but no one would do anything to her. My next move was to grab my backpack and head straight for the door. Soon I walked back into my bedroom, sat on my bed and wondered why I did what I did. It made sense at the time.

The next week I went to Community College to sign up for classes to get my diploma there. Things got muddled at registration and I wound up in a class taking their final exam. I sat down, took the test and passed with a 98. My high school years were over.

My word though, you have no idea how much I regret the decision to leave school without speaking to you. You used to tell me that you would work through issues with me, but I suppose that shame and embarrassment overtook my thoughts. This may turn out to be one of the biggest regrets of my life.

All that I can say now is that I miss you more than you could know.

. . .

Alan

CHAPTER NINETEEN

Oh Alan, I was so glad to get your letter in the mail today. I've been so worried about you that it's kept me up at night. Getting to sleep at night is almost impossible when the person that you cared for the most just vanishes. That's what it feels like, you were here one day and gone the next.

I heard about what happened in your English class. That was bullying, she had no right to embarrass you the way in which she did.

Will you please call me? I want us to stay in touch and plan on doing things together. Just don't vanish from my life, please Alan. Call me. Please.

Molly

CHAPTER TWENTY

Dear Alan,

It was great to see you again last night. For some strange reason I miss you the most at Christmas. When you called and told me that you had a present for me, I felt as if Santa had brought you to me. As usual I have a gift for you. This year it's something very personal and you even asked for it one day when we were together.

Let's try to exchange our gifts the day before Christmas Eve. I can come to your house or you can drive out here. Either is good for me. I'm excited that I'll get to see you again. Maybe we can spend some time together before you have to go back home.

Molly

CHAPTER TWENTY-ONE

Dearest Molly,

I remember asking you about a Bible and now I have my very own. The "Time In A Bottle" that you wrote in the Bible is encouraging. You still look to your future and see me in it with you? That warms my heart and brings some peace to my soul. How in the world did you remember me asking about a Bible that I could understand. Thee, thou and thy type words just don't help when I am reading and trying to understand what a writer is saying,

Why do I miss you so much at Christmas? I've tried for the past three years to figure that out and still don't know the answer. You're on my mind daily during other times of the year, it's just that at Christmas I want to be with you. I want to go on long walks with you, hold you close to my chest, kiss you and just hold your hand. One of the great mysteries of my life I suppose. Maybe one day I'll figure this all out.

There is some kind of attraction that keeps pulling me back in your direction, like a magnet. No matter how far apart we are I can feel that emotional tug in my soul that wants to pull me back your way. Could it be that it gets stronger at Christmas? There is no one else in this world that I have ever felt that connection with.

There are so many things in life that I still don't understand, but I want to know about love, I don't understand love at all. Is it just physical or just emotional or mental? Could it be all three wrapped up into one package deal. A movie came out a few years ago and in it someone said, "Love means never having to say you're sorry."

That makes no sense to me at all. It makes love seem like some magic that takes all of your troubles away. Suppose I love you and step on your toe, I don't have to say that I'm sorry?

What if Christmas is about love more than Valentine's Day? That may explain why that thing between us becomes so strong and I have to see you at Christmas. I'm sorry if I am rambling while writing, that's just the way my brain works. I have to know "why" about anything that I don't understand.

I hope that you have a great New Year.

LOVE,

Alan

CHAPTER TWENTY-TWO

Dear lost boy,

You are so smart and you can't figure out what love is about? You're right when you say that we've talked about this several times before. I think that you know what love is and what being in love with someone feels like. I also think that maybe love just scares you because it's new to you.

Think about this. Have you felt these same emotions with other girls that you have dated? What about the first girl that you dated, you told me name was Cathy. How did you feel then? Did you say, "I love you." to them? Why? What did you mean when you told them that? You know the answers to those questions.

I would be embarrassed to say this if we were sitting somewhere talking, but it's easier when I write it. You probably told those girls that you loved them so that you could be intimate with them. Have sex, sleep with, lay with or be intimate are all the same. Sometimes boys think that the three magic words to get a girl in that predicament are, "I love you." If girls need that type of relationship with a boy to think they are being loved, I feel sorry for them. They are just trying to replace a missing emotion with something physical. That is exactly what you are doing!

I'm sorry for being so blunt and to the point. That has been on my mind ever since you told me that you struggled with the meaning of being in love. Alan, I love you but I don't need anything from you to validate that feeling. For me it was love at first sight and I have loved you since that day. Just spend some time thinking about all that I just shared with you. I love you.

MOLLY,

How did you become so wise at such a young age? I am amazed at the words that you send to me. Exactly what I need to hear! I may not like what you tell me or maybe uncomfortable with it, but you simply tell things like they are.

I wish that I could see you again before a weekend day rolls around. Going to school to sit and talk during your lunch period is probably not my best idea, but I think that I would do it if that was the only way to see you. Sad that I have to work and couldn't get to the school anyway.

Thanks,

Alan

CHAPTER TWENTY-THREE

Molly,

I'm sorry that I didn't call you or try to get together with you last weekend. It's all so sad and stupid on my part. I wonder how you are doing, I miss you, I tell you that I'll call you and I don't do anything that I say I will. My weekend was a mess and I was blind sided by something that happened.

You probably don't want to hear this, but Katie and I aren't seeing one another anymore. This is something that I thought would happen soon and it's the way that it came about that hurt the most. She and I were going to get together last Saturday night. Nothing special, hanging out. That morning she called and wanted to change our plans. She said that she was going to get together with her friend and that her friend was going to spend the night with her. Not so!

Turns out that she had been seeing someone else and they were going out that night. I suppose that I should have been shocked, hurt, sad,mad or had some great show of emotion. The event did make me stop and take a look at myself and my life. Really, he has his own car and I have to share one. He has money to take her out and I have to try and help the family financially (what little I can). I think that he's still in school while I'm struggling with what to do next with education. I've made many comparisons between me and her new boyfriend, it was meant to be this way. Ah well.

She has been an aggravation to you and now that will cease, no more "hang up" phone calls. You had told me that she and I didn't seem to be compatible and you're right.

We lived in two different worlds and I can see that now. There is no way that what she and I had was love though, I don't know what else to call it. Were we in like with each other or just needy and clingy?

It seems as though it's been ages since you and I have seen one another. It may seem like bad timing to say this but I still miss you. This is something that you should hear my voice telling you and I realize that. If I had not isolated myself from you then I could be telling you this. When I left school I separated myself from almost all of my friends and I regret that. I used to imagine us seeing each other each morning before class and during lunch and even after school. In my dreams I thought that when people saw you then they would expect to see me at your side. Dream big dreams right?

Would you consider going out together some night soon? Of course you may be seeing someone else and I understand if that poses a problem. I just feel the great need to recenter my life and you are on my mind so much that you may be at the center of my wasted life. To be totally honest, I am lonely in this world. There are people around me and even old girlfriends but I still feel alone. I've no idea where I belong in life or what I need to be or even who I really am inside. It all gets too confusing some days.

I love you,

Alan

ALAN,

I was surprised to get your last letter and even more surprised when you called. Don't feel alone about being confused with yourself, I feel that way most days. It's like I told you when we were at the park last week your confusion makes me feel even more confused. Where do I stand in your life, who am I to you? There are many nights when I quieted down from the day and as I think about us I tell myself that I know what the truth is. The real truth must be that I'm just not good enough for you. That is what I should have told you at the park and I wanted to tell you. When we are together something happens and those thoughts change. You make me feel like you love me and I feel free to tell you that I love you. When we're together, everything seems to be good.

I didn't tell you this while we were together but I have been seeing someone else. As a matter of fact when you called and asked about going out, I left him hanging. I just ditched him so that I could be with you again. He's a nice guy but has to come from out of town to see me. That fact went right out the window when I heard your voice on the phone. I would probably do it again.

Thank you for telling me about you and Katie. You seemed to be relieved to tell me that she started seeing someone else. I know that you'll be happier and can start to focus on your own life. You used the word isolated in your last letter to me and that was the exact way that I feel about us sometimes. What you did was exactly that, you walked away from everyone who liked you. You feel alone and what you did brought that onto yourself.

You have no idea how much I want to be part of your life and to help you get through your hard times. I'll do anything to help to show you what love feels like and what love looks like. How do I make you see that?

It was good to hear you talk about college and your future. I've told you many times that you are too smart to not pursue further education. You can do anything that you want to when you set your mind to it. You obviously think things through and figure stuff out, reaching your own conclusions. That is a gift just don't forget that it's your gift.

You can call me whenever you need to, if you just want to hang out or go to the park or whatever. I'd really love to go back to that lake in the country with you someday.

TAKE CARE,

Molly

CHAPTER TWENTY-FOUR

Hey! How have you been? I know, I know, I should call you but I just don't feel like I deserve to just barge in on your life right out of the blue like that. Hearing your voice would be great but I've done nothing to deserve hearing something that wonderful. Letters seem much easier for me when I try to say what's on my heart. I can erase things that don't sound quite right or come out all wrong. Somedays I wish that my life had an eraser. It would be so good to take away the foolish things that I've said to you, just a couple of rubs and they would be gone forever. I remember that you wrote to me that you would like to save time in a bottle. Well, I'd love to have some of that time back with you there at my side. If you do find yourself with some of that time you saved would you mind sharing it with me?

I've told you before how I think of you daily and wonder how you are or even where you are. This past weekend I saw you for the first time in months. You wouldn't know this but I'm working at the drug store near your old bakery job. Somehow I landed a job working in the pharmacy of all places. It's a good place for me simply because the pharmacy team that I work with keeps encouraging me to get into college. Every week it seems like that topic comes up and they've become good mentors to me.

If you remember the pharmacy in the store is in the back and up higher than the rest of the space. It's easy to see who's coming and going from back there. Saturday evening while I was working I glanced at the front entrance and was stunned. It was you and Cathy coming in and you looked like I had never seen you look before. I'm sure that I was standing there staring at you and you were more beautiful than I had ever seen. Just the way you were dressed, your hair and the way that you smiled stunned me. Every bone in my body wanted to rush down to see you and be with you even if only for a moment. I didn't. I walked to a space where I knew that you couldn't see me and just watched. When you left I realized that I had been an idiot and should have at least said "Hello." to you. But, I didn't.

The rest of my weekend was hard. I had let the person that I need the most walk away again and you had no idea that I was there. I'm my own worst enemy at times and this was a classic moment. I depress myself by not doing what I should do.

I was supposed to go out with someone that I work with that night, but called and cancelled. Some lame excuse came up and I stayed to myself that evening. Later as I was lying in bed I was listening to some music and realized that what I had done was to break my own heart again. I'm certain that I've done that to you so, I guess it was time that I did it to myself. Being alone was the most painful place that I could have been that night. My loneliness was multiplied and my sadness was magnified, it was just me who had to face it.

I still am in awe of the way that you looked. It seems as though it was yesterday when you were in jeans or denim shorts. You were beautiful then but even more so now. When did we start to grow up? I still feel like the boy you met in school. I walked away for what seems like a moment and it's as though you transformed overnight. Maybe I shouldn't be surprised, we're all going to grow up one day.

ALAN,

You saw me and didn't say hello? I wish that I had seen you while you were working, that would've made me happy. Not to see you working, but just to see you. Did the girl you were going out with know the real reason that you cancelled your date? You must have called her at the last minute since it was almost 7:00 PM or so when Cathy and I stopped by the store. I always like seeing and you know that. After all of the times that I've told you that you have to remember. You asked me once if I was still saving time in a bottle to spend with you. I am and I will keep doing so.

Love to see you,

Molly

CHAPTER TWENTY-FIVE

Molly, thanks for spending some time with me on Sunday afternoon. Early spring is one of my favorite times of the year and being with you made that day even more special. Something in my life changes when we're together. Those feelings that I have for you grow stronger and it seems as though all is right in the world again.

My problem is that I don't know what my problem is. Does that even make sense? When I look back at my life I see a boy struggling with being loved and feeling affection from anyone. As a young man I probably try too hard to find those qualities in the wrong people.

A thought just popped into my brain that has never taken up space in my mind before. You have never pursued me, not once! How very odd that I should think of that now. Even when we are together and alone you have been the perfect lady. That thought actually brought out a question. Have you ever wanted to pursue me or have you pursued me without me knowing? Perhaps I'll never know.That was a big change of topics for such a short letter. I had to ask you before I forgot about it.

HOPE TO SEE YOU SOON,

Alan

CHAPTER TWENTY-SIX

Dear Alan,

Have I pursued you? Do you mean in real life or in my mind. I may have gone out of my way in school to make sure that I see you. Clinging to you or following you around like a puppy, nope. That's just not how I was raised. I'll be honest with you, I have pursued you for what seems like a million miles in my dreams. When we are together and you have to leave for home I dream of begging you to stay. There are times when I lay awake at night and think of calling you or just showing up at your house unexpectedly. I've even prayed for you and, selfishly, asked for you to know how much I love you. Remember my dream about us getting married? I do and maybe I will have to be patient!

You'll never have to thank me for spending time with you, I love being with you. One of these days you'll see just how much you mean to me.

Understanding you is difficult and I'm glad that you continue to share your thoughts and feelings with me. Hearing the burdens on your heart helps me to know you on a deeper level. You're special Alan, God created you to be smart and funny, don't ever change. I love you just the way you are!

Molly

CHAPTER TWENTY-SEVEN

Dear Molly,

I hope that everything is going well for you. Earlier tonight I was reading through the notes and letters that you sent to me over the past years and wanted you to know how much I cherish each and every word you've written. We've been writing to each other for a long time.

The words that really hit me in my heart are when you speak of things that I have said and done to make you sad. I wrote it to you before, but it bears repeating...I'm an idiot. I say things that should never leave my mouth. I trust that someday you can forgive me for making you so blue.

Alan

CHAPTER TWENTY-EIGHT

Dear Alan,

I have all of your letters tucked safely away. They get pulled out on a regular basis so that I can do just what you did, sit and remember our time together. Having these to reflect upon helps me get through those times when I miss you most. Our times together are always special to me, I wish that I could see you again. Creating more memories of time spent together would be incredible.

I've been working at a men's clothing store after school and on weekends. Most of my time working is at night and not getting off until 9:00 PM and by that time I am exhausted. Cathy and some friends of ours go dancing on weekend nights. You remember that I love to dance? You should join us and try it some night.

Always remember how I feel about you. If you need me just call.

LOVE,

Molly

CHAPTER TWENTY-NINE

Molly,

I heard that you've graduated! Congratulations! Even though I was able to finish school early, I envy you. Walking up to receive my diploma in a cap and gown would have a great feeling. Although I did march to receive my diploma, I marched to the mailbox, opened a lovely golden envelope and inside was mine. I would have been proud to watch your ceremony.

I called you a short while afterwards and found out that you had gone to the beach to celebrate your liberation from school. Immediately I knew that I should have been there with you. Sadly my thoughts drifted to thequestion, "Who is going to protect you from the potheads and drunks?" That, in my mind, was my responsibility! Ah yes, delusions of grandeur!

My graduation trip was a bit more subdued than yours. After I took my diploma from the mailbox I went to work. My manager at the drugstore let me drive his new Pontiac Bonneville for two days and it had a CB radio to play with. I had to take him to the airport and pick him up when he came back from his trip. He had no intention of paying for parking, so I had a new car for a few days.

CHAPTER THIRTY

Back to your beach trip. Hearing that was one of the worst things that has ever happened to me. As soon as I hung up the phone my brain delivered tragic news to my heart. My brain knew that I had probably lost you forever and all that my heart could do was break. After my years of confusion and hurting you with poorly chosen words, this is what I deserve.

The saving grace at that moment was in the Bible that you gave me and I went into my room to read those words from your own handwriting. As soon as I opened the cover the words leapt out at me and seemed to envelop my heart. You wrote:

If I could save time in a bottle, I would save it for me and you.

I know where those lyrics came from and I also know that you had buried them in your heart. They were written in my Bible so that I would bury them into my own heart. Those precious words will stay with me into eternity.

LOVE,

Alan

CHAPTER THIRTY-ONE

Dear Alan,

I'm not making fun of you, your letter was beautiful and heart-felt. It sounds as though you may be just a tiny bit jealous and I find comfort in that fact. We've been apart for months and if you feel the way that you described, there has to be room in your heart for me.

No one mentioned that you called while I was at the beach. I've been back for a couple of weeks and this is the first that I have heard about it. It had to be my sister or one of my brothers who answered the phone that day. My Mom would have written a note so she wouldn't forget to tell me you called. Believe me when I tell you that it would have been a big deal with Mom! She's told me that she doesn't understand why I still have such strong feelings for you. It's hard to explain to her.

I wish that I could tell you this next information in person. Since we don't see one another I wanted you to find out from me. I have started dating someone and I think that you may know him. His name is Richard and he told me that you were in junior high together. He acts like he doesn't care for you very much but can't tell me why, not that it matters to you I'm sure. It breaks my heart to tell you this, but I need to be honest with you. I can't tell the future but maybe that could be you and I someday.

I'm in college and working so I don't have much free time anymore. Commercial Art and Fashion Design are my focus areas. We only recently started class but I'm going to enjoy studying about things that I love to do.

I look for you on campus, but there are so many students here that it would be difficult to find you. Maybe we can have lunch together one day. If you look for me then I'll look for you!

Love,

Molly

CHAPTER THIRTY-TWO

Molly,

Thank you for telling me about the guy that you are seeing. I remember him from my junior high days. He and I had some classes together and what I know about him came from them. We were never friends and since you're seeing him I doubt that we will ever be. It was not a shock to hear that you are seeing someone, the fact that it was Richard was the shock. When I was dating Katie a few years ago you told me that she and I were total opposites. Now it's my turn to say, "You two are total opposites, what are you thinking?". There is no room for me to talk though after the crap that I put you through. There is no way that you could ever know this but I get jealous and when I read your letter, that old green eyed monster came out! But I have no grounds to be jealous because I brought this upon myself.

I haven't dated one young lady regularly since Katie. One evening last weekend I listed each of their names and beside the name I made short notes. It was an exercise for me to see how ridiculous and fruitless my relationships have been. If you ever saw the list you would think that I was some lothario but it has not been like that at all. The list made me wonder why I wasted my time and could have been with you all along. You see Molly none of those young ladies could meet the standard that I have set. Not one of them came even close. That was probably unfair, no not probably it was completely unfair and biased. The standard that they had to meet was you!

Now,I am afraid that I am too late.

That must have sounded odd and confusing to you. Looking in hindsight it was odd and confusing for me and I'm the person who came up with the judging standards. I would go out with these girls once or twice and by then I had made up my mind. Let me give you a few examples. I went to a park with one young lady and I just ran across a field so that I could feel the wind in my face. She kept walking and when she caught up her first words were, "I don't like to run,can we just walk?" Another young lady was pleasant enough but I kissed her and it was like licking an ashtray. One told me that she, "didn't like that country, southern rock music that I liked. Not even that James Taylor dude. I only listen to hard core ,shake the walls, rock music." Now you can see what my dating life is like. Pitiful!

. . .

I HOPE to see you again,

Alan

CHAPTER THIRTY-THREE

Dear Alan,

I'm sorry that it has taken me so long to write back. My life is hectic and chaotic with work and school. As I read your most recent letter for the third or fourth time I am still in shock from the things that you said. You've become pretty good at opening up when you write and you express yourself very well. Perhaps you should consider being a writer. I love reading your letters, I actually get excited when I see a new one in the mailbox.

You told me that I am the standard by which you evaluate the girls that you date. I never saw that coming! When did that all start? A long time ago you told me that I was special and unique. If that is still true, you will never find someone exactly like me. It's true when it applies to you, there is not another Alan in this world, only one you. I have spent the past few years convincing myself that I am not good enough for you. That's the reason that I gave to why we never stayed together for very long. Now you tell me that I am better than anyone else that you've dated. I am humbled and flattered by your sentiments. But where are you?

I love you,

Molly

CHAPTER THIRTY-FOUR

My dear Molly,

It happened again! I have a part time job at a grocery store that has me working odd hours. This past Friday I was stocking shelves in the store and something caught my eye. I turned and, to my surprise, you were the object in my peripheral vision. Shocked and taken by surprise I just stood still and watched you as you walked out the door. Once again,I did not pursue you to try and say hello. Once again, I am an idiot! What my heart was telling me was to run after you as fast as I could. Don't wait, you fool go and get that woman. As you well know, I just watched as you drove away. By the way, you look great!

CHAPTER THIRTY-FIVE

Molly,

I did something this past Saturday night that you will never know about unless I send you this letter. Seeing you while I was at work last week ignited a deeper feeling towards you. I can't describe the feeling that I have in me now. The only other time in my life that I have experienced this feeling was on the first day that we met and our eyes locked. The feeling is almost as if an outside force is directing my emotions. I don't know much about God, but could He or would He be so close that he saw the need to intercede in our relationship.

Before I go on any further I have to tell you that I have been seeing someone on a regular basis for quite awhile. Her name is Karen and we met one evening while I was at a hockey game. She is younger than us and lost her father from a heart attack several years ago. Even though I see her a couple of times during the week that feeling that I have for you is just not there. Anyway I wanted you to find out about her from me.

Back to the original reason that I am writing to you after all this time. When you left the store where I worked that day I just stood and watched you drive off. When you were out of sight I realized the sorrow and sadness that you felt when I would go home after we had been out together. One of the deepest regrets in my life is that I made you feel that way. You had no idea if it would be a day or a month if you would see me again. That is a terrible burden for you to have to carry.

Saturday evening, I did something that I never could have imagined. I was determined to see you, no matter where. Figuring out the best probability of where you would be was not difficult. It was Saturday night, you like to dance and the best dance club in town is the Tree House so that would be my destination.

I waited until a little after 9:00 and headed over there. My brain kept telling me that I was being a stalker, but my heart told my head to shut up. Heart won that debate! To see if you were at the club I drove through the parking lots looking for your car. It didn't take long to find it so I parked my car and prepared to insert myself into your world. I waited for just the right moment and I waited some more for another right moment. I argued with myself over how to react if you were there with another guy, dancing closely and every other bad thing that could happen. I would be embarrassed since I don't dance, so I came up with an exit strategy. Crank up the car and forget that anything ever happened. With a great deal of remorse I pulled out of the lot and just drove around town for an hour or so and then turned towards home. My plan was crushed and I had crushed my own heart again.

CHAPTER THIRTY-SIX

Oh my Alan,

I can't believe you went to all that trouble and never came inside to find me. That was sweet of you to want to see me that much.

I don't think that I've ever told you that I moved out of the house and was renting a duplex. It all happened quickly. Richard's sister was looking for a roommate and I was ready to leave home so I moved in with her. I think that he liked the idea so that he could keep an eye on me. That seems like something that he would do. I just don't feel like this housing arrangement is going to last very much longer. The same is true for my relationship with him.

That explains why you saw me at your store, my duplex is less than a mile from there. I wish that I had known you were there, I would have tracked you down in the store just to see you again. Alan, I still think of you every day. I just can't get you out of my mind and I don't want to get you out of my mind.

The next time that you see me please come over and at least say hello. It would be wonderful to see you again.

Love,

Molly

MOLLY,

You called me! Sunday afternoon was one of the best times of my life! I could have stayed on the phone with you for the rest of the day. I could have jumped in my car and sped away to see you. The only thing that kept me from doing either of those was the fact that Karen was at my house. When we talked it was as if no time had passed since we had last seen one another. There were hundreds of things that I wanted to say to you. Your voice sounded so beautiful and soothing that I could have listened to you all afternoon.

I loved it when you asked me if I had someone with me because I had totally forgotten that Karen was in the other room. She could have been standing in the doorway listening to our conversation for all I know. She stayed in the living room watching tv with my family. The only thing that mattered to me was that you were on the phone. It was a one hour slice of the time you are saving in a bottle for us.

Karen did ask me who I had been on the phone with for so long. All that I could say was that it was a very dear friend whom I had not spoken to in a long time. That was the only thing that she asked. Other than the big question which she had just launched my way. "Well, was it a girl?" I was not going to lie so I said yes, it was a girl and just a friend. I asked if she had friends who were male and she picked up on my point.

CHAPTER THIRTY-SEVEN

I can't wait to see you on Saturday evening. For the first time in ages we will be alone together to talk and laugh like we used to. As we discussed, no pressure to do anything but get to know one another again, enjoy Christmas lights in McAdenville and enjoy each other's company.

Thanks again for calling me! By the way does your Mom know that you called me? I remember that was one of her rules, girls do not call boys.

"When the final line is over and it's certain

That the curtains gonna fall

I can hide inside your sweet, sweet love forever more."

. . .

Alan

CHAPTER THIRTY-EIGHT

My dear Alan,

Saturday evening was incredible! Seeing the whole town lit up in green, red and white was breathtaking. I didn't even mind the traffic stand still, it just gave us more time to catch up on our lives. I would love to come here every year.

I must confess something to you, nothing bad mind you. I have told myself all week that I would not tell you that I love you. No matter what the circumstance, those three little words would not be spoken by me. No way, no how. To tell you that I love you meant that I was setting myself up to be hurt again. That would not happen.

Standing by the lake and seeing lights reflected on the water was serene. I heard the wind in the fir trees and the children in the cars as they rode by where we stood. I was happier than I had been in a long time. Then you kissed me! Not just a peck on the cheek kiss, this kiss was long, and slow. After we kissed, you hit me with a love bomb. Your eyes had penetrated my soul and when you told me that you had never stopped loving me and said, "I love you." Do you remember that I answered you immediately? I was peering into your eyes and said, "I love you Alan." All of my defenses were crumbled and in my mind I was asking myself why I said those three little words. I realized immediately that I said them because it was the truth. I have loved you since our first glance in high school and I will always love you.

CHAPTER THIRTY-NINE

By the way, you may have figured this out but Richard and I are no longer seeing one another. He ambushed me with the news that he was going out of town with an older woman. I became irate because of all the crap from him in the past and I became angrier than I have ever been. He had the gall to make me promise that I would not start seeing you again. He said, "You can do much better than him." Anger level increased!

ALL MY LOVE,

Molly

CHAPTER FORTY

My precious Molly,

I will never forget Saturday night with you! That was the kind of evening that, I think, that we have both longed for. Thank you for telling me about your "no I love you" plan. My plan succeeded! As soon as we made plans to drive to McAdenville, I started thinking about the evening and being alone with you. My vision for the night was to make sure, before I took you back home, that you would know how much I love you. The atmosphere was perfect for a time in which we faced the truth. That truth is we are in love, have always been in love and will always be in love with one another. The only way that I could do that was to love you like I have never loved you.

Stopping at the lake was a part of my strategy. We could leave the car to walk around the giant glowing Christmas trees, not much talking but taking long looks at one another. Staying focused on your brilliant blue eyes and, when the moment was right I would kiss you. Not a lip smack kiss or a quick kiss and quick hug done together. I planned on telling you that I love you after we kissed. I received what my heart desired, you confirmed that you were still deeply in love with me. You, my dear, are an incredible kisser!

The ride back to your house was ecstasy and saying good night was agonizing.

CHAPTER FORTY-ONE

I am going to Karen's house to put closure to our relationship, if she will speak to me. When she showed up at my house Saturday just before we left, I was completely taken by surprise. I'm sorry that you had to hear that, it went as well as it could given the circumstances. All that I wanted to do was take your hand, walk to the car and be alone with you.

My heart is light, my head is spinning and I know why. The strong love that we share is a powerful force and is strong enough to bind our souls forever.

I LOVE YOU DEEPLY,

Alan

CHAPTER FORTY-TWO

Alan,

Our relationship today is what I have been dreaming of since 10th grade! I have known all along that I am in love with you and believed that you loved me. We just took different paths to get to where we are today. You are not the same person that you were in high school. Listening to you let's me know that you know what you want out of life as well as what you need to walk away from. My mind had been made up to be patient and wait for you. The fact that you loved me was very clear. The fact that you had become confused about life and love was clear as well. I've told you many times that you are unique, funny and smart. I hope that you never stray from those traits that make you who you have become.

Needless to say that my Mom is shocked about us. When I called you that Sunday afternoon she walked by the area where I was talking and I told her that it was you on the phone. Her response was simply, "Well what does he want?" She's going to love you when she gets to know you.

I love you,

Molly

CHAPTER FORTY-THREE

My love,

I'm still trying to figure out how a movie can have such a profound impact on us. There was something about going to see A Star Is Born that completely captivated us. We were close and quiet during the movie, we held hands on the way back to my car. Remember, you had worked that day and we went directly from the store to the theater, a walk of about 100 yards. Side note, I love being close and quiet with you.

This is where the words, "profound impact" come into play. We drove the entire 7 miles to your parents house and no words were spoken at all. Nothing. We just rode, held hands with an occasional hand squeeze, but neither of us said a word. I pulled into the driveway and we sat for just a few more moments of silence. After those moments, do you remember what happened? You should since you were the instigator of what happened next. Very casually you leaned towards me and very quietly you looked into my eyes. You had a small tear making its way down your cheek. You said, "Alan, I love you and I will love you forever."

While I was still stunned by what had just happened you leaned in and kissed me. It was, without a doubt, the most soulful kiss that I have ever experienced.

My only thought was, " I will never lose you again."

CHAPTER FORTY-FOUR

There is a song in the movie that probably stirred our hearts more than anything. I only remember some lines from the first and last verses and that is due to the fact that I was probably in sensory overload. If couples had theme songs, this would be ours. If I recall correctly the words are something like, One love that is shared by two I have found in you. Thank you for loving me so well,

Alan

CHAPTER FORTY-FIVE

Alan,

That whole night was saturated with our love. I was happy to see you, happy to go see the movie with you, ecstatic when you told me that you love me. The ride back home was quiet, all that I could think about was you and I and all that we have been through, yet there we were, totally in love.

The tear that you mentioned was a tear of joy. I had anticipated kissing you, but the words that I spoke were spontaneous. There was no inkling that I would say them until after I had said them, if that makes sense.

Seeing your words, in your handwriting saying, "I will never lose you again" brought great warmth and comfort to me, a peace to my soul. After experiencing what we've been through since I called you that Sunday, I have decided that it was worth the wait. Seeing you struggle and mature all the while struggling and maturing myself was amazing. We had the privilege of watching one another from a distance and not many couples can say that.

I LOVE YOU ALAN,

Molly

CHAPTER FORTY-SIX

Dear Molly,

I think that I have figured out "love at first sight". Sitting in a quiet place and thinking has become one of my favorite things to do. It became a habit in the midst of the confusion and chaos in my life. Actually I started this practice in the 11th grade. One Saturday evening I found myself in a transcendental meditation class. That should tell you something about how fun my life was while we were apart! That is a long story but I did learn the virtue of sitting in the quiet and pondering life's issues.

Love at first sight is an immediate emotional connection between two individuals whose eyes meet one another's and they continue to remain locked in. No words need be spoken at first, that will come later. Somehow the eyes and facial expressions communicate love for the person you are looking at. Perhaps almost an awakening in which your senses ignite, your emotion gets fired up and all that you can see is the person in front of you.

I have nothing to base that on other than the first time that I saw your face. You captured my attention without saying a word, you were sitting at your desk looking like an angel. In a split second you turned and looked at me as though someone tapped you on the shoulder and whispered, "Psst, take a look at that guy staring at you." As soon as you faced me I knew that something extraordinary was happening, something that I had no control over. Funny thing is, I didn't want to stop looking into your eyes,ever.

A new and wonderful sensation swept over me. It felt warm, secure, caring and eternal. I knew that I would get to know you and that our lives together were going to be special. For the few moments of contact I can recall thinking, " I hope that she is going through what I am going through right now, if not I'm getting ready to make a fool out of myself later today".

That my dear is when I fell in love with you. The sad part of this is the fact that I had no idea what to do with my emotions. Having never experienced pure unconditional love before was like receiving a wonderful gift with no instructions on how to use that gift. I had to figure that out on my own and with your help. It was you who showed me what to do with this incredible gift and I am forever grateful.

I love you,

Alan

CHAPTER FORTY-SEVEN

Molly,

Hopefully this can help explain what I was trying to tell you over lunch today. Your brain was preoccupied with your store's inventory and I'm sure that the details didn't register with you. This letter will let you understand why I am moving out of my parents house. Please don't feel bad about being lost in your thoughts, I understand.

Dad came into the bedroom that my brother and I share today, and without warning, told us that we had to move out and find our own place to live. The part of that conversation that is most troubling to me was his final statement. His exact words were, " We can't afford to keep you here anymore, you need to start this weekend looking for a place to move." I don't know how my brother felt, but I was stunned.

That's what I was talking about today. I'm still stunned, but I have to look for an apartment to share with others. It's either that or go buy a bigger tent. This may turn out to be one of the best things that could happen to me.

LOVE,

Alan

CHAPTER FORTY-EIGHT

Alan my love,

Hello. I love receiving your letters and little love notes, they let me know that you're thinking of me. I got home from work around 10:00 PM and am still keyed up from work. I decided to stay awake and write to you. I think that you have sent more notes to me than I have to you. I'm no exception to the fact that everyone loves getting personal letters in their mailbox.

There is something that is troubling me and writing it down will help me organize my thoughts. At times I will say what I don't want to say or I will not say what I really want to say. Many times I've walked away from conversations thinking, "Well Molly you did it again", What they heard was not what I wanted to say. Time will pass by between that person and myself, we'll get busy and I'll forget to explain what I said.

Our relationship has taken some strange twists and turns since we met. You and I are in love, there is no doubt about that. Whatever path you have veered on has always led you back to me. I've said it before, we were just meant to be together.

My friends used to tell me to "Get rid of him!" only because they have seen

the times when I was sad, angry or hurt because of someone that you had done. Each time I'll tell them that they don't know you the way that I do. Holly is probably the worst of my friends to say that. You had done something while we were still in school and her solution was, "Take me to that jerk's house and I'll kick his butt for you!"

I am telling you about the past simply because I have a thought that tickles my brain sometimes. It tells me that I can't trust you or that you're going to walk out of my life the way that you used to. I couldn't face that again.

Alan, I love you and you alone. It's you that I need and you that my heart desires. Will you be patient with me as I build up complete trust in you? Do you recall when I told you that I was not going to tell you that I loved you? We were by the lake watching the Christmas lights. I was adamant that I wouldn't utter those words only because I didn't want to get hurt again. Somehow those little words were said and I realized at that moment that I could trust you with them.

I've said a great deal only to tell you that there is a tiny part of me that is working on not being afraid that you will leave me again. Each day that we are together, each time you make me feel loved, that feeling fades away. I'll never bind your conscience over this, that's who I am. I'll never manipulate you because of this, that too is not who I am. I do believe in the power of love and I promise to love you well. Someday soon it will be gone and it's the love that you give to me that will defeat it.

THANK YOU FOR LOVING ME,

Molly

CHAPTER FORTY-NINE

Lovely lady,

What a wonderfully open and honest letter! Meshed into all of those words was the message, Alan I love you. It was great to receive, great to read, and re-read, and re-read again. True honesty is a thing of great beauty!

After I called you to let you know that I received your letter I decided to respond in kind and send you a letter. I love writing to you.

Trust is earned, it is not given. I have a track record of being too easily distracted in this busy world and when that happens I forget to do what I promised. History can be one minute ago, one year ago as well as one thousand years ago. My history by which I am trusted or not trusted spans only the past few years. I created my history and I can remember that history and decide that I will not repeat it. We will have a new history written together.

Our past was a foreshadowing of our lives today. I used to tell you that I loved you as a friend and now you are my closest friend. I told you that you would be a good wife for some man, now we dream that perhaps that man is me. I would also tell you that I loved you and I have discovered that you are the love of my life. I promise to love you well.

I AM in love with you,

Alan

WELL HELLO! I enjoyed our time together yesterday evening. It seems as if we have fun no matter where we go or what we do. Whether we're at a park, at your parent's house, or in a restaurant we always wind up laughing. Molly I love just being with you, it makes my heart happy.

I JUST HAD a great flashback to (I think) our first date. When I told you where we were going and what we would be doing you just gave me that beautiful smile. The thought of sitting on a loading dock and shooting at rats in the city dump would have brought forth a frown, pout or the stink eye from most young ladies. Your smile and eyes told me that you just wanted to be with me. It was a great time, in part because we laughed so much. I can be in total funk and you know exactly what to do and snap me out of my self hosted pity party.

WE WERE SO busy goofing off last night that I totally forgot to tell what happened at home. I can't recall ever being angry and frightened at the same time. You told me one day that I am one of the most laid back people you've ever met. If you had been at our house when I became angry you would have either thought that I had dual personalities or just walked away. I made a beeline straight into the house and hunted down the instigator of my wrath. Pity the fool who got in my way!

I CLEAN our car before we go out, I can't stand to be in a filthy vehicle let alone invite someone to ride with me in the midst of trash. Anyway, I opened the trunk of the car to get a can of oil, I got the shock of my life. Scattered over the floor of the trunk were orange pills. Hundreds of them! It was my Dad's pain medication, Darvocet, and it is highly illegal to have them with you if they have not been prescribed for you.

IMAGINE what could have happened if I had not opened the car's trunk. I could see being pulled over for a minor traffic violation. Then the officer looks in the trunk and in mere seconds our date would have continued in the back seat of a squad car. They would been in my possession and since you were riding with me you would be an accessory to the FELONY DRUG POSSESSION charge.1

THIS IS the kind of messed up stuff that I have to deal with at home. I am thankful for being able to complete my plans for a highly romantic first date.

I LOVE YOU,

Alan

CHAPTER FIFTY

Dearest, I would have gone almost anywhere with you back then. You are the first guy that I loved and I just wanted to be with you. My brothers were jealous and wanted you to take them to the same place the next time you go.

When I read your letter and heard of the drugs I couldn't believe what I was reading. Going out last night after having just read your letter helped me keep questions fresh in my mind. Imagine having to make a phone call to my Dad and ask if he would bail me out of jail on a felony drug charge! It would have been a long, long time before he'd let you see me, we would have to plan a secret rendezvous place.

The other night you asked me how I was doing and I said, "Fine." Well, thank you for calling me out on my answer. You know my moods, my up days, my down days, when something is bothering me that's incredible. You even decode my facial expressions and the time in my voice. Taking time to get to know me that well shows how deep your love is. No one knows me like you do. Sometimes I think you can read my mind and know my thoughts. I'm thankful that we have such a strong bond between us.

REMEMBER THAT I LOVE YOU,

Molly

CHAPTER FIFTY-ONE

My dear Molly,

I'm still reeling a bit over the promotion offer that you received. You're good at what you do and your managers seem to notice that. While I am proud of you for the job opportunity I am frightened by the fact that you will be three hours away. You're a beautiful lady and I know that other men notice you. I've watched them flirt with you in your store and I want to intervene to put a stop to it. At those times I just have to put my jealousy aside.

When we were at the lake enjoying the Christmas lights, we kissed and you told me that you loved me. I made a promise to myself. That vow was that I would never lose you again. I feel like I may be doing just that now. I didn't get to sleep last night, my mind was flooded with thoughts about both of us getting lonely. My imagination takes over when I think of all that could happen and I become even more sad. I love you and I trust you. It's other men that I have no trust in. The thought of living without you is painful. Actually having to live my life knowing that I had lost you would be an impossible burden to carry. I have to follow my promise that I will not lose you again, no matter what it takes.

I LOVE YOU,

Alan

CHAPTER FIFTY-TWO

Alan,

I'm so sorry that this is making you sad. When we were together last night and started to talk through everything we both wound up being sad. I mean what I told you, if you don't want me to go, then I won't. This is just a job and nothing more. There are other jobs out there and I can always get hired by another company. Tommy told me that the store here would be my stop after Raleigh was up and running. You were right when you said that we only see each other on the weekends here now.

Love, you say that you don't want to lose me again. You're not going to have to worry about that. I'm glad that you can go apartment hunting with me and Mom. That will be a fun day trip and I just found out that my Grandma is going with us. I want you to be part of this time in my life simply because it's your life too. By the way, I worry as well. I wonder what girls are going to start chasing after you once they find out that I live out of town. I'll be working 12 hour days when I first open the store and will be dead tired after that. If you're in class and working you'll probably be in the same situation. Please do something for me. I can't believe that I am asking you for this, the thought just popped into my head. Will you guard your heart while we're apart? There are going to be people who tempt you and people who don't want us to remain together. I love you.

Molly

HEY LADY, I've been thinking about the end of your last letter and began to fixate on something. We can talk more about this later, but I wanted to put this note in your purse for you to read later.

Wherever I go around this side of town there is a good chance that someone who knows me will see me. It happens frequently and I'm not complaining because it keeps me on my toes! That brought up the question that I want to talk about later. When you're living 3 hours from me, who will be your accountability? Who will help you to not get caught up in a compromising situation? There is one person that sticks in my mind when I think of this and I don't trust him at all. I really want to talk through this before you leave.

. . .

I LOVE YOU,

Alan

CHAPTER FIFTY-THREE

My love,

Yesterday was a long day of riding, but it was worth it. The apartment that you decided upon is great. While walking around the parking lot I felt safe. I'll rest better knowing that you're in a place like you chose.

While you, your Mom and Grandma were talking I decided to keep quiet and enjoy the family conversation. Your Mom was asking about next steps with your company, I anticipated the possibility of moving back home to run the store here. What you told her next floored me and I'm glad that I had been quiet because it was all that I could do to not shout out, "What the hell are you talking about?" Had I asked about the information that you gave to your Mom it would not have been a quiet conversation.

In the midst of a sad, stressful time in our relationship you brought her up to date on the possibility of you moving to New York to take a position as fashion designer. New York City?!

I know that you have a full plate, preparing to move and to open a new store while still maintaining your regular job, but why had I not heard about this other job possibility? My first thought was that you were giving up on us.

I don't even know how to start a conversation about this. That is why you are reading this in a letter first. Remember, I am in love with you.

HEY SWEETIE! I have to tell you again that your concern about my accountability warmed my heart. You care about me and you show that in ways that are unexpected. Sometimes I believe that you don't realize that you're caring for me, it's just a part of who you are. I'm thankful that we can sit and talk about things that concern us. You're a great listener, I believe that you would sit and let me talk all night. I would sit and talk all night just to spend time with you.

As for New York, that is well off into the future if it happens at all. I don't even know if I could live in that city. Please believe me when I say that you are much more important to me than going anywhere. I love you.

Molly

CHAPTER FIFTY-FOUR

Dear Funny Lady,

One of the hardest things that I have ever had to do was leaving you Tuesday. Three long lonely hours to make it back to the last place in the world that I want to be. I left and you were crying. You can't imagine how many times I stopped to turn around and hurry back to you. When I got back to my apartment there was no one else at home. The other guys were both working so I just sat down and started this letter. I'll mail it tomorrow and you'll receive it in two days. That's what the mailbox sign said!

We have been through quite the journey since that first day of 10th grade. I am convinced that there is a Divine intervention in our lives. A force that drew us together with one glance, that created a love stronger than either of us has ever known. One day

I will know how to ask "Why?" but for now I'll enjoy the great gift that we've been given and I will love you deeply.

I will not be working on weekends as long as you are so far away. After class on Fridays my car will be heading north and back to you. I'm sure that you'll have to work during those weekend days and when you do I'll drive straight to your store. If you are working on Saturdays I'll drive you to work, have lunch and dinner with you at the mall. Sunday will be spent just enjoying being in love with one another.

Nights will be the most difficult time for me. After class and work are over I'll be at the apartment alone for most of the evening. That time will be consumed by thinking of you, missing you, worrying about you and being glad that you love me the way that you do.

We will make this long distance relationship work, there is no doubt in my mind. I am already anticipating Friday and holding you in my arms once again. You are the love of my life.

I LOVE YOU,

Alan

CHAPTER FIFTY-FIVE

Alan,

I decided to put notes in your backpack while you are with me. That way they will be waiting for you to read anytime after you leave on Sundays. Waking up next to you is so beautiful. I love that I can turn my head and see the one that I love laying close to me. Alan you bring peace to my soul like I have never known. I remain convinced that God brought us together and will continue to deepen our love for one another. I miss you and am looking forward to Friday and the time that we will be together again.

I LOVE YOU,

Molly

CHAPTER FIFTY-SIX

My love,

Do you remember how it feels to wait all year for Christmas and when that time finally arrives it's over much too quickly? That is how my weeks feel. I am anxious for Friday to get here so that we're together again and on Sunday afternoon I am in shock that our time together is over. I still hate seeing your tears as we say goodbye once more.

I found out that it is good for me to write to you on Sunday nights when I get home. It helps me to process the transition from being with you back to being with a couple of grungy roommates. Plus, it gives me a chance to connect with you during the middle of the week.

In one of your letters you mentioned the temptation that people will place in front of you when they realize that I am not living there. Let me tell you, lover I had a strange temptation when I got home today. There was light left in the day and I decided to go for a run. When I made it back to the apartment I was going back in through the front door. As I made my way up the sidewalk someone said "Hello!" to me. I looked to my left and saw a lady dressed in a tight black outfit and walking three cats. You know that I am neighborly and as you'd expect I waved and said, "Hello." Then with the three cats on leashes leading the way, she headed my way.

CHAPTER FIFTY-SEVEN

By now I figured out that something was amiss! She said "Hello! My name is .... and I'm your new neighbor. I'm out trying to meet the people who live around me. Would you like to come over to my place for a drink and dinner? We can get to know one another." Molly, I promise that this is true and here's where it gets even more weird. Cat lady turned to her right just a wee bit and I saw something move. She turned a little more and I found myself staring at a woman dressed in a tight black outfit who had a tail! My next move was to head into our apartment as quickly as I could move.

Once I was safely inside I lost it! I was laughing so hard that I thought I was going to wet my pants! My imagination ran amuck with thoughts like, "Would we be having MeowMix as our main course?" and " Were the greens that she would serve really catnip?" or what if I excused myself to use her bathroom and she told me, " Why yes, just head down the hallway and it's the first room on the right. Little litter boxes are for the cats and the big ones are for us." I'm going to be cracking up about this all week.

Dear, I miss you and I hope that this letter brings some joy to your week. Remember that I love you and that I will be there as quickly as I can on Friday.

LOVE,

Alan

CHAPTER FIFTY-EIGHT

My love,

If you're reading this it means that you are on your way back to your apartment and that I'm missing you. Why don't the weekends last longer, why do they have to go by so quickly? When we're together my world seems to be a better place and I'm at peace. While you're here my countenance changes and the chaos stops. All that I do during the week is work and sleep. I'm at the store from 10:00 AM until 10:00 PM then I drive home to an empty apartment and get ready for bed. Honestly I've thought about buying a fold up bed and just staying in the store overnight sometimes.

Alan, I miss you! I love you and I need to be where you are no matter where that is. You keep me grounded and help me stay focused on the truly important things in life. Being separated like we are has caused me to realize just how much I love you. I can't wait to see you again on Friday.

Molly

CHAPTER FIFTY-NINE

My love,

I thought that after a while leaving on Monday would become easier on us. Driving back home is not hard. Getting in late after the drive is not hard. Seeing tears running down your face makes me more sad than I have ever known myself to be. I think about all of the times that I broke your heart and caused you to shed tears, now it seems like I'm doing it once again.

It was nice to have Sarah riding with me this week, at least giving me someone to talk to. We all were emotional wrecks as she and I left you. After I dropped her off at your parents house I headed straight to the apartment. Thoughts from our weekend are still fresh in my mind and I wanted to capture them before they slipped away.

The thoughts that have the place of prominence in my heart are about our love for one another. Those feelings grow deeper by the day. Occasionally I will catch myself lost in daydreams, thinking of ways to stay with you or to bring you home with me. I've gone so far that some days I mentally work on plans to transfer schools, get in my car and just show up wherever you may be. Then we remain together and do away with Sunday afternoon tears.

CHAPTER SIXTY

Sarah told me about your Dad stopping by your apartment the Monday after we moved you in. She laughed as she told me about him seeing my car in the parking lot. Apparently he just turned around and left to continue his business trip. Honey, if he had knocked on your door I would have had a heart attack!!! He and your Mom began to wonder if we had secretly married. I would love to be able to hear that conversation.

Molly, when we were talking Saturday night I had no idea that I would tell you about my secret fears. Once the first word slipped out I knew that I had to open myself up to you. The dreams of you getting tired of being alone and finding someone else who loves you seem too real. Thank you for understanding and calming my fears. I am glad that you shared your fears with me as well. How ironic that our hearts are knit together and we both have the same fears. The look that was in your eyes told me that I had nothing to fear. It was a look of pure love. You speak so well with those lovely blue eyes!

As soon as I tuck this letter into an envelope I am going to scour my backpack for my notes from you. Each week I look forward to these love notes from you, they help me as I begin to face a new week without you.

I LOVE you more than you could ever know.

Alan

CHAPTER SIXTY-ONE

Alan,

I'm preparing to face another week of 12 hour workdays and then onto another night alone. All that I need is you here with me. I lay in bed at night wondering what it would be like to have you here to kiss me goodnight and then to kiss me good morning for each day of my life. Selfishly, I want you all to myself. I despise being alone now and after longing for you to be with me for so many years, this just doesn't seem right and it's not fair.

Will there ever be a day when you don't have to leave me? A season when time will be our time. A day when I can redeem the time that I've saved in a bottle just for the two of us.

You probably don't want to hear this but I have to be open and honest with you. Sometimes guys who work here in the mall come to the store and just hang around to talk. I have these fleeting thoughts wondering if there would be any harm in having lunch with one of them. Then I think of us and my promise to you that I would not put myself in a compromising situation. You are the only man that I want and the only man that God has set apart for me. I am deeply in love with you.

Molly

CHAPTER SIXTY-TWO

My love,

I missed you and was excited that Friday had finally arrived. Did you have to begin our time together with an announcement that some other employment opportunities had come up in your company was troubling. When the only specific location named was New York City, my heart sank. You know how I feel about that, we've talked about it before. Then on top of that to be told at the last minute that you had work on Sunday and that your manager,Tommy would be working with you I was undone. We had so little time together that I wondered why I drove up there. Molly, I've seen the way that he looks at you and flirts with you, even if I'm in the store. Whether he's married or not he's up to no good and you'll be in a closed store all day on Sunday. Ironically, that is the day that I go back home. Please tell me, if you will, why is this not a compromising situation and who will hold you accountable?

The whole drive home seemed to take forever and my mind kept going to places that I should not have allowed it to visit. I kept thinking, well is this the beginning of the end for us? Will she have to work next Sunday? When will she be offered the position in New York? Would she want that job so badly that every other thing in her life will take a back seat?

My thoughts were fueled by fear, jealousy, and sadness. I am fearful of losing you, I can't explain that adequately but just know that I love you. Would you please try to schedule yourself off on Friday afternoon? I need to hear your laughter. I need you and I'll get in my car and drive to you tomorrow if I have to. I simply need you.

DEAR,

I realize that you'll be back home when you read this, but I need to apologize for the weekend. During the week I missed you and, without thinking ,took the weekend away from us. When I was getting ready for work this morning the reality of what I had done hit me hard. Sometimes I get tunnel vision and can only see that task that I have to complete.

I can imagine you back at your apartment sitting down to write a letter to me. Receiving the letter will be nice, I look forward to opening them. What you have to say in the letter is my concern. You have been so faithful to drive up here each weekend and I couldn't handle it if you weren't here with me for those days. I love you.

Molly

CHAPTER SIXTY-THREE

Dearest,

I never mentioned this to you and on my way back home today I heard a song that struck a chord with me. When we were driving up to look at apartments you told your Mom about New York. There was a song playing at just that same time. As I was sitting beside you trying to keep your surprise news from wrecking me, I concentrated on the music. Late in the song these words were sung "Don't give up on us."

I still struggle with that conversation, your words seem to haunt me. It's as though little pieces are plastered in my mind. Words such as transfer, fashion design, dream job and the worst, "Tommy said that..."

This past weekend didn't seem the same as the others when I drive up. Maybe we were both just tired. My week sucked and I know that you stay busy, I just don't know. I was glad to see you, no, I was relieved to see you. Sometimes our brains will hang on to the most negative side of a conversation and this was one of those times for me. I have a fear deep inside that I'm going to lose you. This week you could get a call with an offer to go anywhere that your company has a location.

CHAPTER SIXTY-FOUR

I grow weary of the things that go on back here. We need to be together no matter the place or season. Even when I'm at work people will point out this girl that I should date and when I'm polite and explain our relationship it riles me even further to hear "She'll never know.". Karen came by the bowling alley and asked me to "take me away, Kip is beating me." I was way out of my Mr. Nice Guy personality and abruptly told her to just "leave, that's not my problem." Call the police, not me." I feel as though I am stuck between two worlds. There is this world with school, job, meddling family and loneliness and the world where you are. That world is almost like a fantasy. For a brief time I am with the one who loves me. I wake up in the mornings in that world and my day is made perfect because you're beside me.

Next Friday night can we just spend the time focused on us and our world? No work, school, or family discussions, I want to talk about you and about me and our lives together now and in the future.

This was long, but I have a lot weighing on my mind. Just remember that I love you.

Alan

CHAPTER SIXTY-FIVE

Alan,

Once again if you're reading this note it means that you are back at your apartment. Honestly, I love sending these notes home with you and I love writing them, but I hate sending and writing them as well. When writing I can share my heart with you in a small way. When writing them I know that you're leaving soon and it makes me start to miss you even before you leave.

Are we okay? You seemed reserved and quiet this weekend and it made me stop to consider what you have to go through each week. My job has consumed me. All of the hours that I have to work piled on top of the stress that it brings added to what you have to deal with has me worried. I worry about you and me in this long distance relationship. At times it all becomes too hard emotionally.

I will promise to spend more time focused on us during the weekend. What that sentence should have said was, "spend that time focused on you." We are at one of those times in life where we have to make decisions that could change our lives. Are we in a place where we are able to make decisions together? If this long distance gets to be too much for me you'll be the first person that I run to. Will you please tell me that you will do that as well?

This was going to be a simple, short and sweet note to remind you that I love you. It took a different direction but I hope that it says the same thing, I love you.

SWEETIE,

I have more to say so I thought that I would surprise you with a second love note. Hopefully you'll find this since you may only be expecting one note.

Alan, I have loved you since our eyes first met. After all that we have been through and all of your words that left me wondering, I still love you. As I write those words I realize that I love you even more today than I did then. Through our years together and time spent apart we've laughed, played, danced, loved and wept together. There have been many nights when we wept alone over things that most people would not understand. But we always came full circle, back in each other's arms.

In my first love note tonight I asked you if we are okay. You are probably just reading those words and I hope that they stay with you and cause you to think while we're apart this week. I am going to expose my heart and make myself vulnerable in the rest of this note simply because I love you and we need to find out if we are "okay" and can make it through the distance that separates us.

CHAPTER SIXTY-SIX

First and foremost,I love you. Throughout your times of doubt when you struggled to express your love and to accept the love that I gave you, my love for you grew stronger. While we kissed by the lake of Christmas lights my love for you grew stronger. While we were sitting and talking in your sister's single wide mobile home my love for you grew stronger. While I watched you drive away leaving me alone for the first time my love for you grew stronger.

If our love is true, we can weather any storm. I firmly believe that The Lord has set us apart for one another during the turbulence of the times of doubt.

You worry about me because I'm alone and I worry about you because you're alone. We love one another, but we haven't learned to fully trust one another. We both know the damage that others can do to us and to our relationship. We also know others who would do that damage if they sense the opportunity. We both know that we have to talk and work through our fears. I am thankful for weekends when you drive up to spend time with me. That is the time for our relationship to become stronger and we learn to fully trust one another while falling more deeply in love.

CHAPTER SIXTY-SEVEN

Oh my dear sweet love,

How much have you and I gone through to get to where we are today? I am thankful for our reunion on Friday and I am sad to be back home once again while leaving you alone again. I have never been more anxious and excited to see you than I was on Friday. The weekends always seem to pass by too quickly. It would be wonderful if we could make time stand still occasionally. We could make our days together last much longer and spend more time with no distractions or interruptions. If I had a magic lamp and was allowed the three wishes that fables mention, one of my wishes would be to spend more time with you.

You are an amazing lady! I think that when we were discussing your letter after dinner on Friday I realized that I had committed it all to memory. My school would have been much more productive if I could have been as interested or committed more information to memory. Truth is that I read your letter so many times that if I had not memorized it I would begin to wonder about my brain power diminishing.

Trust is a powerful word and I am thankful that you brought it up so that we could examine trust in our relationship. In an earlier letter I mentioned that trust is earned and I don't take that for granted. It's ironic that I write of trust being earned when, after all that I have been through in my life, I have trouble trusting most people. That has never been the case with you. You have always been open and honest with me and I've never had problems trusting what you say or even who you are. That is a rare character trait!

I have a wish for us, or maybe it's a dream, but I think of it often when I am alone. In that dream we're laying in bed in the evening and we just talk. We share our deepest desires and our long held secrets, just as we fade away to sleep we realize that we are about to miss one of the most important events of our day. We stop, kiss and say goodnight and as we drift off to sleep a peaceful calm descends on us. When we wake in the morning the peace is still upon us as we stir. Our goodnight kiss has now become a good morning kiss to start our day. One day that will be our reality and I long for that time to come quickly.

Writing this and seeing those words before me makes me miss you more than I do already. Now all that I have to look forward to is sleeping on a sofa and dealing with two smelly, noisy room-mates coming in after midnight. That is a strong dose of reality!

I LOVE you and I need you in my life.

Alan

CHAPTER SIXTY-EIGHT

To my future bride,

I decided to sit and write this letter just as I would if it were any other Sunday and I had left you in tears as I drove off for home. As I drove to see you today I rehearsed my lines for what seemed like a thousand times. The four words that are so easy to say, but carry so much weight. Two lives were changed forever tonight with the whisper of five powerful words, "Molly, will you marry me?" You took only four words to make the life change complete, you sweetly smiled and answered, "You know I will." And in a matter of minutes two souls that have been bound together by love will legally be bound together in the church before God and man.

The moment just before I asked the big question was one of the most fearful moments of my life. There were a million thoughts racing through my head, the most prominent of them all was, "What if she says no?" Sadly, the question did not come with an answer. If you had answered with "No" I would probably have remained motionless hoping that I misunderstood you.

Molly, after all this time I can't believe that we are going to fulfill the dream that you had in high school. When you shared that dream with me I was overwhelmed with a sense of, "I think that she may be right!" What I felt for you then was love and what I feel for you today is that same love that has been magnified and matured. It grew over the years and blossomed into something of great beauty. Everytime that I saw you the fragrance of that love followed.

This time I won't leave on Sunday only to leave you behind. You won't have to watch me drive away, praying that I make it safely back to you on Friday. We'll depart together, our hearts full of joy and laughter and eager to see your family so that we could share our happiness.

The job timing is incredible. You're coming back home to manage the store where you began your career. When we talk about our lives together and all that has happened to keep us together, you always bring God into the conversation. You trust and believe, I need to follow your lead and get to know Him like you do.

Last night will be forever etched in my mind. I swore to myself that I would not lose you again. If you left me it would be because I pushed you away. Yesterday evening marked the end of our long journey and the beginning of a new life together.

Molly, I am in love with you!

Alan

CHAPTER SIXTY-NINE

Love,

Friday night? Asking me if I would marry you on Friday night? Were you so eager to propose that you couldn't wait? Friday night when I had worked all day and just wanted to be at the apartment and relax with you? Friday night when my week of missing you was over? Friday night was the perfect time to ask me to marry you!

I just realized that I don't have to write notes to slip into your backpack. I don't have to write to you, but I'm going to continue to write to you. Even as we're together I'd like for you to write to me. Your letters lift my spirit, encourage me, and are another way to tell me how much you love me. Please don't stop!

We're getting married! I'm going back home! Life is good! It will be interesting to hear what my old friends say when they find out that I am marrying you! Remember I told you what Richard said as he broke off our relationship? He tried to make me promise that I would never get back together with you, the jerk. I hate to tell him but you were on my mind everyday that I was with him.

There will be a lot of people who will be shocked that we are marrying. We can talk about this on the way home, but the biggest shock will be in my family. Imagine the look on my Mom's face when she hears the news. My Granny will have a conniption fit when she hears, I'm going to let you tell her! Then there is my Dad and that is the big talk that we need to have. You'll need to ask his blessings on marrying his daughter and that makes me nervous. We'll plan that while we drive. You've made me happy, love!

MY LOVE,

Soon there will be a day when we won't part company at night. We'll finish our day and go to sleep side by side and awaken side by side. Now that your Dad has given me permission to take your hand in marriage. "I reckon that'll be alright. If you can handle her." was his way of saying "Why of course you may take my daughter's hand in marriage. Welcome to the family, son. May your days be prosperous and your nights filled with ecstasy." I still can't get over how nervous you were as soon as we walked into the house.

I'll tell you what I'm not going to do this coming weekend. I'm not driving three hours to see you, leave on Sunday and hate the tears running down your face, and drive three hours back to an empty apartment. Those times were well worth any sacrifice just to see you and I would continue that routine for as long as had to if it meant that I could be with you. This week my three hour drive home will be with you in the car with me.

Molly, it feels like a dream when I think about us getting married. I think about your dream and your confidence that we would be husband and wife one day.

A long time ago I wrote a letter to you and in that letter I said that you're different and unique. You still embody those traits and I still admire them in you. I've never met anyone with your passion for people. When you like someone it is very clear and when someone has wronged you that becomes very clear to that person.

You love hard and you love well. When you tell me that you have loved me since that first day, I have no doubt about your statement. Molly, your whole heart and soul were behind the word love. Even when we didn't see one another for weeks and months, you loved me. Your love for me never died, though your thoughts and emotions may have been tucked away for safekeeping, they remained alive and well. When it looked as though we would never make it as a couple, I have no doubt that you never stopped loving me.

THANK you for waiting patiently for me.

Alan

CHAPTER SEVENTY

Sweetie,

I was reading through some of your old letters last night and I came to realize a couple of things. A long while ago I told you that I would love to save time in a bottle and spend that time with you. That was during a period in your life when I had no idea when or if I would ever see you again. You would call me to go out with you. I always said yes, and we would have a wonderful time together. The words that you would leave with me typically were, "I'll call you"or "I see you soon." Both unintentional half truths or lies, I'm just not sure. When you were absent from my life is when I would begin to save time in a bottle. When all is said and done at our wedding I want to redeem all of the time that I have saved. I'll give it to you in exchange for every day for the rest of our lives.

I don't know if you heard what Granny said on Sunday. While we were in the kitchen she asked me how you were treating me and I told her that you we're behaving and being a good boy. Her comeback was typical for Granny, but this time she wrecked all of us. She looked at me and had a mischievous look in her eyes and said, "Well he's cute and if you want to dump him let me know. I'll call him up and invite him over. The first thing that I'll do is straighten his butt out! You can have him back after that."

Welcome to my family!

ALL MY LOVE,

Molly

HELLO LOVE,

After the comment from your Granny, maybe I need to start copying her in my letters to you. She's a teasing little tart, I would bet that she was a hot mess back in her day!

I can't believe that in a few weeks we will be married. The word has spun around work down at the bowling alley. Karen came by last night and kept walking by the counter as if she was stalking me. She made me feel uncomfortable, but I just let it roll. I guess that she was working up the nerve to speak to me, and she finally came over. When I took a break I went over to the bar and had dinner. She saw me there and just strolled right over to my table and acted surprised when she saw me. The only words out of her mouth were, "I saw your fiancé, she's beautiful. I guess I'm not good enough for you, am I?" With her piece having been spoken she stood up and walked away. It was a strange encounter.

THAT NIGHT MUST HAVE BEEN my night to take a shot at. When I left the bar I walked back to the office and, of all people to see, I ran into her mother. Looking away from her did no good. As I passed by I heard her say, "Why aren't you marrying Karen? We all thought that you would and were counting on it." That was an easy question to answer. It may hurt some feelings but it was going to be the truth. Straight and to the point I replied, "I am marrying the love of my life" and I walked on.

That evening was rather odd, but it was bound to happen eventually. It felt good to say that I am marrying the love of my life. The love of my life. What if I had missed marrying the love of my life? I can imagine that I would spend the rest of my life wondering why I let the love of my life slip away. My life would have been spent agonizing over my grand mistake of letting you go. My love, I think about this often and I am so thankful that the love of my life will be by my side for the rest of my days.

We're getting so close to that day that I find myself wanting to ask if we can just leave together, go to the Magistrate and have a simple civil ceremony. That would most certainly be selfish, but most certainly make us both happy. I love you and want you by my side.

ALL MY LOVE,

Alan

CHAPTER SEVENTY-ONE

My love,

At times like this I'm glad that we decided to continue writing to one another. The time that we get to spend together is wonderful, but sometimes late at night I can't sleep and writing this letter feels like I am talking to you. I can't wait until we can lay in bed and talk all night into the wee hours of the morning.

It's funny that Karen was at your work the other night, the vultures are starting to circle overhead. If they only knew how alive and vibrant our love is. When Richard came into the store, I knew right away that he was intent on causing trouble and just being the ass that he always is. I loved the answer that you gave Karen's mom and I used almost the same one on the jerk.

Remember when I told you that he tried to make me promise that I would not go back to you after he said "You can do better than that." referring to you. The bright spot of my day is when I looked him in the eyes and told him that I was marrying the most wonderful man in the world who has always been the love of my life. Then I walked away.

It is so close to our wedding day that I almost can't stand it! Just know that I love you more than you can imagine, I have always loved you more than you can imagine and I will always love you more than you can imagine.

FUTURE MRS. AUSTIN,

I am going into a strange new phase of my life. We are getting married and I've never been to a marriage before and I don't know what it will be like. I don't think that I'll know how to act and I don't know how you will act. Will our personalities change, will the way we speak to one another be different? I love you deeply and I hope that our love will grow, but I don't think that there are any guarantees.

I was intrigued with what your Pastor saw in us. During our last meeting he told us that our love for one another would carry us through the hard times. Did he say that he could "See how much we love each other." If goofing off and having fun during a premarital counseling session is a sign of love, then he did see our love in action!

After so much time apart physically and yet with hearts bound so tightly together I have to wonder which caused the Pastor to see our love for one another. You know my personality and my penchant for knowing why and how about things in my world. I'll spend some time at night looking at us to try to see what he sees. If that fails, I'm just going to call him and ask!

CHAPTER SEVENTY-TWO

The closer we get to our day, I find myself wanting to just run away with you. That bossy lady that thinks she is coordinating our wedding is crazy. She actually thinks that she can push you around when it comes to what you want for our ceremony. It's fun to watch her go into "bossy lady" mode where she starts sentences with words like, "you will", "I want", ``We're going to do", and my favorite, "I'm the church's wedding coordinator and we're going to to it..." When those words pop up my radar starts pinging and I want to warn her, "Lady you've got incoming force from the unfriendlies. Either take the words back, run or duck and cover!" Apparently she actually believes no one will challenge her authority. Foolish lady! I've seen it too often, you don't let people back you into a corner.

That was a lot of rambling but I can't sleep and my brain is racing 500 miles an hour, anxious and excited about our future.

CHAPTER SEVENTY-THREE

My soon to be husband,

Funny that you couldn't sleep when you wrote your last letter and I read it after I got home tonight. Now I can't sleep, your excitement is contagious!

I have to admit to you that, though my heart always knew that we would marry, my brain was in doubt at times. There were times when I didn't see you or speak to you for months, my brain told me to quit longing for something that I would never have. My heart would counter with, he'll come back to you for you are the love of his life. It was a strange debate taking place over you and our future together. My friends were like my brain and heart. Some would tell me to let you go and others would tell me to wait for you. As you now know I did both. One Sunday morning I decided to take matters into my own hands. That is the day that I called you!

You mentioned looking into the future after we've married and wondering about changes. Of course there will be change, we grow and mature, we become wiser with our years. One thing that will only diminish if we allow it to is our love for one another. We'll have to be sure that we remain close, nurture one another, encourage one another and find ways to show our love for one another. If we can do those things, our love will remain strong.

As for Miss Wedding Coordinator, we just let her think that she is in charge and then do things the way that we want them to be. Mom just turns her head and looks the other way. She always has plausible deniability. Mom is sly that way.

Just a few more days my love and my dreams, hope and wishes will become real. I will become your wife and then if you leave saying, "I'll see you later,"

and don't come home for a month, I'll hunt you down. When I find you I will bring a whole chocolate cake and feed it to a pack of raccoons while you can only sit and watch. You know that I am exaggerating and would never waste a cake that I just bought and I don't know where to find any raccoons. I said all of that because I trust you and know that you will do what is best for us. I trust you. There was a time when I didn't know if I could say that so easily. When we talked about trust in the past you made a great comment. You said that "trust is earned" and you said it out of your love for me. These past months you have certainly earned my trust.

Molly

DEAR WIFE,

I do. Can you believe it? We said those powerful little words in front of the Pastor, our families, our friends and a church full of people. I suppose that with that many witnesses we have to admit that we are officially married! After all our years of tears, fears and uncertainty love prevailed and brought us to a point in our lives where we said, "I do." In high school you told me that this would happen and in the back of my mind that fact stayed stored away along with my silent response, "I hope so."

When the pastor asked if anyone had a reason why we should not marry, I held my breath. It could have been your Granny, one of your friends, one of my friends who stood and said, "Yes sir, I don't think they should marry!" Alan has been a jerk, Molly can do better than him, wait I still love him/her, could have been the reason for postponing our nuptials. The church, however, was quiet, thankfully.

Molly, there were days when I thought that you were gone from my life for good. I checked the newspaper on Sundays to see if there was a wedding announcement or even a simple engagement piece. Had either of these caught my eye, I would have begun work on a sinister plan to take you away. There was already a plan afoot should you be getting married. I've never told this plan to anyone! When the Pastor asked for objections to the marriage, I was going to stand and announce my objections to the ceremony and build my case from there. A part of my team would rush the stage and distract the groom and groomsmen, sweeping them off into the storage area by the left door. My car would have been parked near the front doors ready to roll. As the men were being incapacitated, my role was to rush the stage, grab your hand, whisper to you that you were the love of my life. My car would have been started so all we needed to do was jump in and take off.

Just as we were pulling out of the parking lot you would lean over and kiss me and whisper to me, "You are the love of my life, thank you for rescuing me, it's you that I love." We would have kept driving until we came upon a small country church. Coincidentally the pastor would still be at church and eager to hold a ceremony.

The last act of my plan was to repeat those powerful, small words "I Do." to one another and the dream would be fulfilled and we would hop in the car and speed away into our future together.

My plan was never put into action, as you well know. Your love for me is so strong that marrying someone else was only a remote possibility. For that. I am thankful. Your dedication and certainty about our future is incredible. I have never seen pure love in action before and must say that with it comes determination. Some may label that as being stubborn, but determination is the best word to describe. You followed your heart, never giving up and never giving in to frustration or discouragement. I know all too well that I was the source of much frustration and discouragement! You endured and never lost hope. You had more reason to rejoice at the words "I do" than anyone, My love you're a fighter and that is one of the traits that I most admire in you. We've got a great life ahead of us.

Your loving husband.

DEAR ALAN,

When the pastor asked me the vow questions everyone was expecting me to answer his questions with "I do." Everything in my body wanted to give him a different answer, something that truly expressed what I was feeling at that moment. A few words that would take everyone by surprise and give them something to help them remember our wedding.

If you had not looked so nervous standing up there with me, I could have pulled it off. You looked great standing with me and I was amazed at how cool, calm and collected you appeared to be. Then I noticed it. It was very brief at first, but after a few more moments it became more evident. Your lip was twitching! Not just a little bit either. When you do your Elvis impersonation you make your lip twitch exactly like it did then. It was great!

Well, back to what I wanted to say instead of the usual "I do." What I would have liked to say was, "I GOTCHA! NOBODY ELSE IS GONNA GIT YOU, CAUSE I GOTCHA!"

Alan, remember what I told you so many years ago? That I was going to marry you? I never doubted what I told you. When we met,I didn't know how or when but I knew in my heart that we would stand on that altar someday. I love you

Your Bride

CHAPTER SEVENTY-FOUR

Dear Alan and Molly.

It has been exactly one year since I joined you in Holy Matrimony and I write a personal letter to each couple that marry. I ask family members and friends to tell me how they think that you are doing and what they have seen when you have been around them during the year. Rarely am I surprised by the information that I receive, this year may be the exception. More on that later.

When the two of you sat in my office for our marriage counseling sessions the whole atmosphere in the office changed. If I was feeling down or just in a bad mood you two would change my demeanor and brighten my day. On the day when we were scheduled to meet I looked forward to our time together. We covered some weighty and serious subjects, even then you had me laughing before you left my office!

Do you recall the time when I told you that your marriage would last for years and years? When you were with me I could feel the "electricity" between you. The way that you looked at one another and even the manner in which you spoke between yourselves told me all that I needed to know about you.

CHAPTER SEVENTY-FIVE

When you told me about your letters and notes that you wrote over the years I was elated. The two of you had already begun to capture the greatest tool for a marriage that can withstand the tests of time. Even back in high school, the power of communicating began in simple notes and it blossomed from there into your semi-regular letters. One of the keys to a successful marriage is communicating between a husband and wife.

Your love for each other is highly visible, someone could spend ten minutes with you and walk away knowing that you two have a rare and special love for one another. I picked up on it the first time that you were in my office!

You two keep on doing what you're doing. I can see you being married for forty or fifty years. I've never met a couple so perfectly matched. When I tell folks about you all that I can say is that God placed you together, there is no other explanation. I am proud to have been just a small part of what God started in your 10th grade class.

ENJOY YOUR LIVES TOGETHER,

Reverend Tucker